Mama's Tamales

Marge Mendoza

ISBN 978-1-0980-9863-6 (paperback)
ISBN 978-1-0980-9864-3 (digital)

Christian Faith Publishing, Inc.
832 Park Avenue
Meadville, PA 16335
www.christianfaithpublishing.com

Printed in the United States of America

Dedicated in loving memory of my daughter

JENNIFER JASON MENDOZA

1996–2020

MAMA: It is such a nice, rainy day. This is a *perfect* day to *make* some delicious TAMALES!

Abuela, Papa, Jennifer, and Jason all agree that it is indeed a *perfect* day to *eat* some delicious tamales.

Mama checks the pantry and finds that she has none of the ingredients needed to make tamales. So she makes the following grocery list:

1. Pork roast
2. Garlic
3. Onions
4. Chili Colorado
5. Masa
6. Lard

MAMA: Now who will go with me to buy the ingredients for the tamales?

ABUELA JENNY: I can't go now. I am much too old to go out in this wet weather!

PAPA: I can't go now! I am much too busy watching a soccer game!

JENN: I can't go now! I am much too busy styling my hair!

JASON: I can't go now because I don't want to!

So Mama puts on her coat, takes out her small red wagon (to load the groceries into for the trip home), and goes to the corner market alone.

MAMA: Now, who will help me prepare the chili, roast the pork, and mix the masa?

ABUELA: I can't help you now! My eyes are much too old to be around all that chopped onion and chili!

PAPA: (*He doesn't answer because he's now snoring* VERY LOUDLY *while napping on the sofa.*)

JENN: I can't help you now! I am meeting my friends to watch a movie!

JASON: I can't help you now, because I don't want to!

So Mama soaks the corn husks in the sink while she slices onions, presses garlic, roasts and shreds the pork roast, and mixes the chili and lard into the masa. She mixes until it is fluffy and smooth to perfection!

MAMA: Now, who will help me spread the masa and the meat onto the corn husks, fold the tamales, and place them into my special *huge* pot for steaming?

13

ABUELA: I can't help you now! I'm too old to miss my late afternoon nap!

PAPA: (*Who was just now awake from his early afternoon nap*) I can't help you now! I'll miss the last half of the soccer game!

JENN: (*Who can't answer because she is sitting in a movie theater, eating buttered popcorn with her friends!*)

JASON: I can't help you now, because... (*Well, you know!*)

So Mama prepares the tamales and places them in the special *huge* pot all by herself.

The entire house is soon filled with the delicious smell of tamales as they steam in Mama's special *huge* pot.

MAMA: I know who will be very happy to help *eat* the tamales now!

ABUELA: (*Who has, just that moment, awakened from her late afternoon nap.*) I will be very happy to help you with that *now*, my dear!

PAPA: I will take several tamales off your hands *now*, my darling wife, if you will kindly serve them to me here by the TV, so I won't miss the ending of this exciting soccer game!

JENN: (*Who is just home from the movie theater*) I am sick of eating popcorn, and *so totally ready now* to help eat tamales!

JASON: I will help eat tamales *now*, Mama, but *only* because *I want* to!

Mama's family stare (with their mouths wide open), as she puts on her coat! They stare as she loads her special HUGE *pot of freshly cooked tamales on to her small red wagon!*

And they stare as she pulls her wagon out the front door, closing it behind her!

Mama simply smiles to herself as she delivers the special *huge* pot of delicious, freshly cooked tamales to the neighborhood homeless shelter…just in time for dinner!

The end (almost…)

Now you can try making your own TAMALES. Mama left you her recipe:

Mama's Tamale Recipe

(Serving: 1 doz.)

INGREDIENTS:

1 ½ cups corn flour
1–1 ¼ cup stock
1 tsp. salt (to taste)
1 tsp. baking powder
10 tbsp. lard
2 doz. corn husks

Cooked and shredded pork roast

Red chili sauce (mix into masa with the broth, and add to shredded meat; amount varies by taste!)

Note: You may also substitute any of your favorite fillings, such as shredded beef or chicken; bean and cheese; potato wedges; veggies; etc.

INSTRUCTIONS:

1. Soak the corn husks in hot water in the sink or a large bowl for at least 30 minutes, until pliable for rolling.
2. Sift together the corn flour (recommend Masa Harina), salt, and baking powder in a large bowl.
3. Add 1 cup of the stock (broth) to the dry mixture; it will be slightly crumbly.
4. Use an electric hand mixer to whip the (room temperature) lard for approximately 2 minutes until "fluffy."
5. Add fluffy lard (fat) to masa mixture in small amounts until all has been combined.
6. Continue mixing until smooth and fluffy; use remaining stock only as needed, being careful not to over wet the masa!
7. Remove excess water from corn husks by patting dry and select the widest ones first.
8. Spread several tablespoon of masa on the inner, smooth side of the husk. (You may either hold the husk in the palm of your hand or place on a flat surface to do this.)

9. Add filling (do not over fill or it will be difficult to close the husk properly).

10. Fold the tamale sides together then fold the bottom narrow part of the husk up.

11. Use a pot with sides high enough that the tamales do not stand over the rim. Add a few inches of water to pot; place tamales on a steam rack inside the pot with open end of tamales facing up.

12. Cover pot and steam on medium to low heat for approximately 2–3 hours, until masa has congealed and is not mushy.

Don't forget! Tamales should always be made for sharing with family, friends, neighbors, and *anyone* who can appreciate the unique DELICIOUSNESS of TAMALES!

(One last thing…)

Did you know?

Homelessness is the condition of people lacking "a fixed, regular, and adequate nighttime residence," as defined by The McKinney–Vento Homeless Assistance Act.

Homelessness is a global issue. The United Nations Commission on Human Rights (UNCHR) estimates that more than 100 million people worldwide are unhoused!

Now…

What do YOU think should be done about homelessness?

For more information on "homelessness in Los Angeles" visit:

https://losangelesmission.org/facts-about-homelessness
https://laalmanac.com
www.usich.gov (United States Interagency Council on Homelessness)

About the Author

Marge Mendoza is a retired childcare director from the city of Los Angeles, with over thirty years of experience working with children, ranging from three months to thirteen years of age. She holds a certificate in Montessori Teaching Philosophy from the American Montessori Institution (AMI) and a bachelor of science degree in business management and organizational leadership from Azusa Pacific University (APU).

As a childcare director, Marge (known to parents and children as Miss Margie) gained insight into the importance of an emergent curriculum through close observation of students' changing interests. She recognizes the value of literature in developing a program that stimulates social awareness, opens conversations, and encourages critical thinking. Through networking with surrounding community organizations, Marge was able to integrate both fiction and nonfiction abstract storylines with concrete situations and real people.

Marge has been blessed with ten grandchildren (Devynne, Alyssa, Michael, Lauren, Joseph, Gabriel, Benjamin, Anthony, Emily, and Noah) and seven great-grandchildren (AJ, Kendyll, Kynslee, Kayden, Kennedy, Francesca, and Maddison).

This book is dedicated to her daughter Jennifer, who was killed in a hit-and-run car accident on February 23, 2020. As a legacy graduate from APU, receiving a BA in criminal and social justice from APU in 2018, Jennifer was a constant source of encouragement, inspiration, and joy to her mother, father, and four surviving siblings, Joshua, Jason, Janine, and Ann.

9 781098 098636